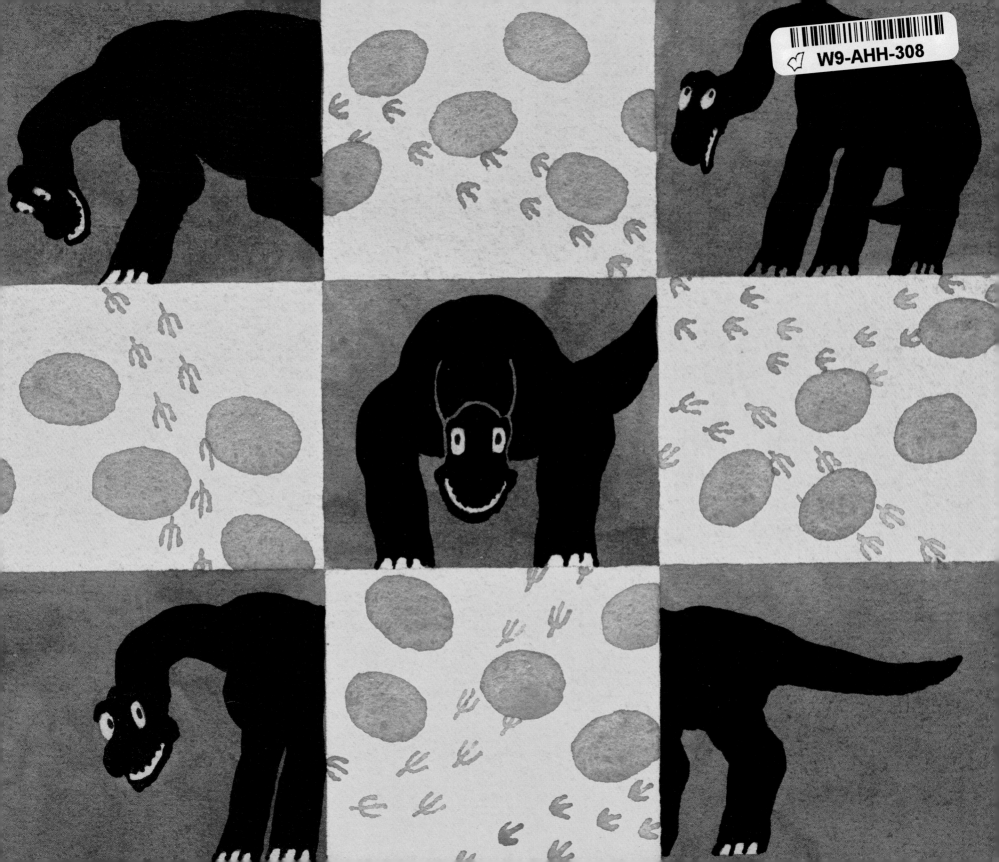

I'M BIG!

KATE & JIM McMULLAN

BALZER+BRAY
An Imprint of HarperCollinsPublishers

Balzer + Bray is an imprint of HarperCollins Publishers.

I'm Big! Text copyright © 2010 by Kate McMullan. Illustrations copyright © 2010 by Jim McMullan. All rights reserved.
Manufactured in China. No part of this book may be used or reproduced in any manner whatsoever without written permission
except in the case of brief quotations embodied in critical articles and reviews. For information address HarperCollins
Children's Books, a division of HarperCollins Publishers, 10 East 53rd Street, New York, NY 10022. www.harpercollinschildrens.com

Library of Congress Cataloging-in-Publication Data
McMullan, Kate.
 I'm big! / by Kate and Jim McMullan. — 1st ed.
  p. cm.
 Summary: A young Sauropod encounters friends and foes while searching for his pack, who left while he was oversleeping.
 ISBN 978-0-06-122974-9 (trade bdg.) — ISBN 978-0-06-122975-6 (lib. bdg.)
 [1. Lost children—Fiction. 2. Saurischians—Fiction. 3. Dinosaurs—Fiction.] I. McMullan, Jim, ill. II. Title. III. Title: I am big!
PZ7.M47879Ijt 2010   2009027206
[E]—dc22   CIP
                                                                                                                 AC

Typography by Sarah Hoy   10 11 12 13 14 SCP 10 9 8 7 6 5 4 3 2 1   ❖   First Edition

For all the cousins, BIG and small: Mimi Knolle, Amelia Owen, Kathryn Knolle, Marie Ellecia Knolle, Grady Kleuser, and Frances Anderson.

Great BIG thanks to everyone at HarperCollins: Alessandra Balzer, Sarah Hoy, Ruiko Tokunaga, and Kathryn Silsand; and to those BIG-DEAL Pippins: Holly McGhee and Emily van Beek.

Huge thanks to Dr. Matthew Lamanna, Assistant Curator of Vertebrate Paleontology, Carnegie Museum of Natural History.

Huh?

You're lookin' at a
super-sorry **SAUROPOD**.
Woke up late,
my herd was gone.

Wanna help me find my pack?
Awright, let's get a move on.

Someone could've nudged me,
woken me up.....

Hey, Stegs—
my pals pass by?
Lemme know
if they show up.

Hmmm . . . where can they be?
I'll see.
Stand back! Elevator?

Going up,

up, up.

Check the neck—

FIVE
STORIES
HIGH!

The weather
up here?
Sunny, with
a chance
of . . .

What's **THAT**?
Rustles in the brush?
Gotta be my herd—

Wait up, guys!

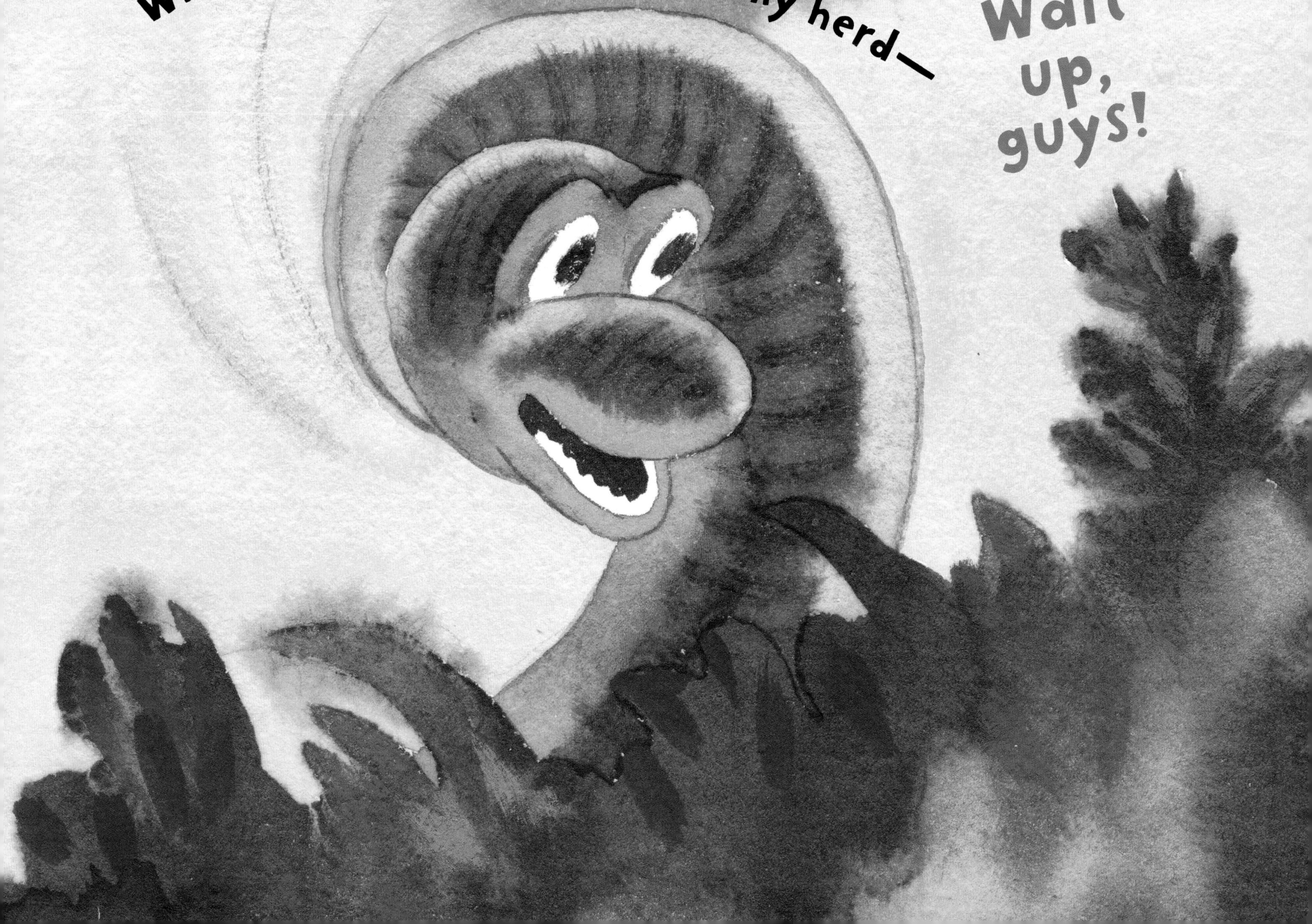

HOLE NOT **DEEP** enough!

ROCK way too SMALL!

Can't hide!
What do I do?
FIGHT?

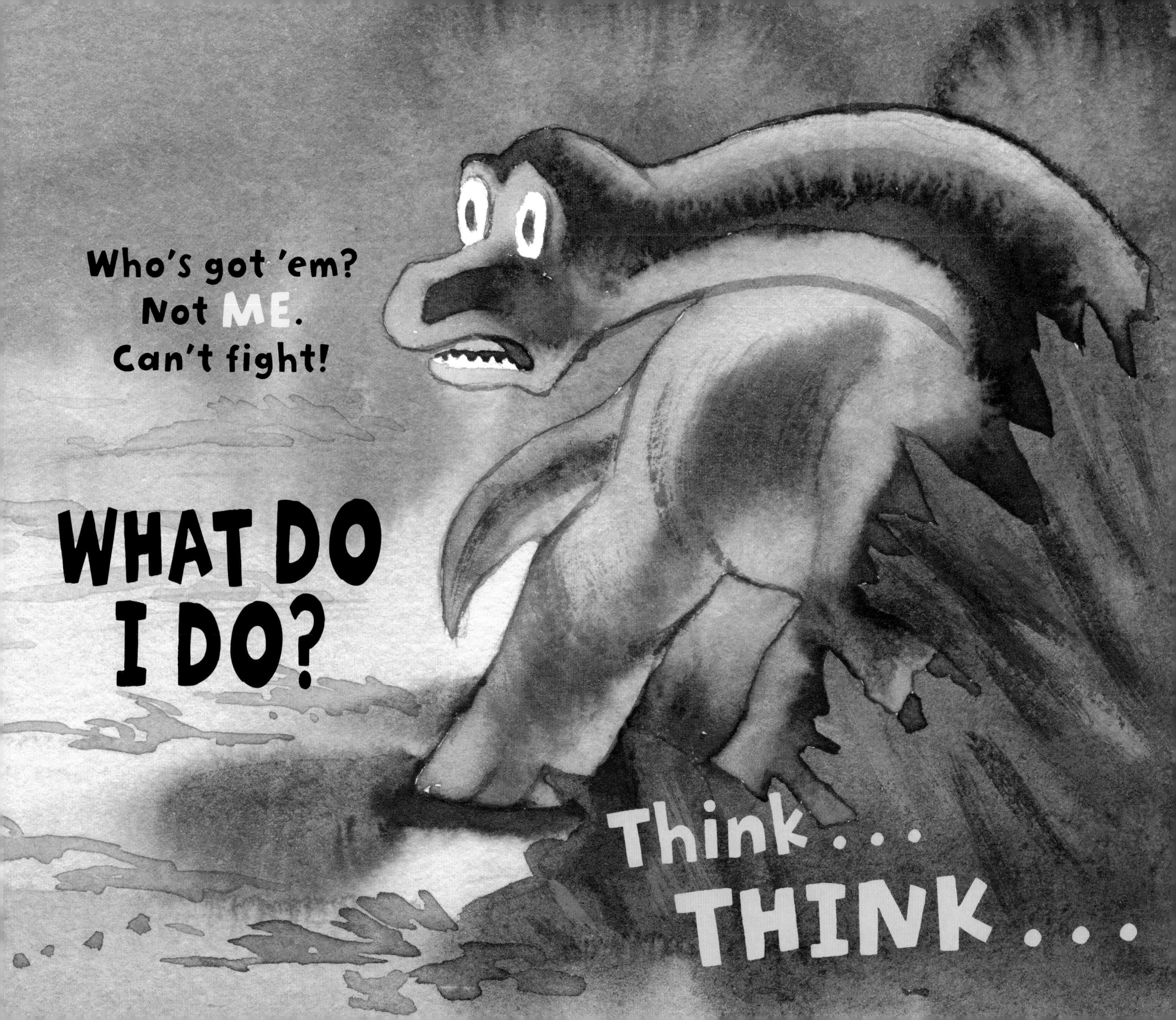

Who's got 'em?
Not **ME**.
Can't fight!

WHAT DO I DO?

Think . . .
THINK . . .

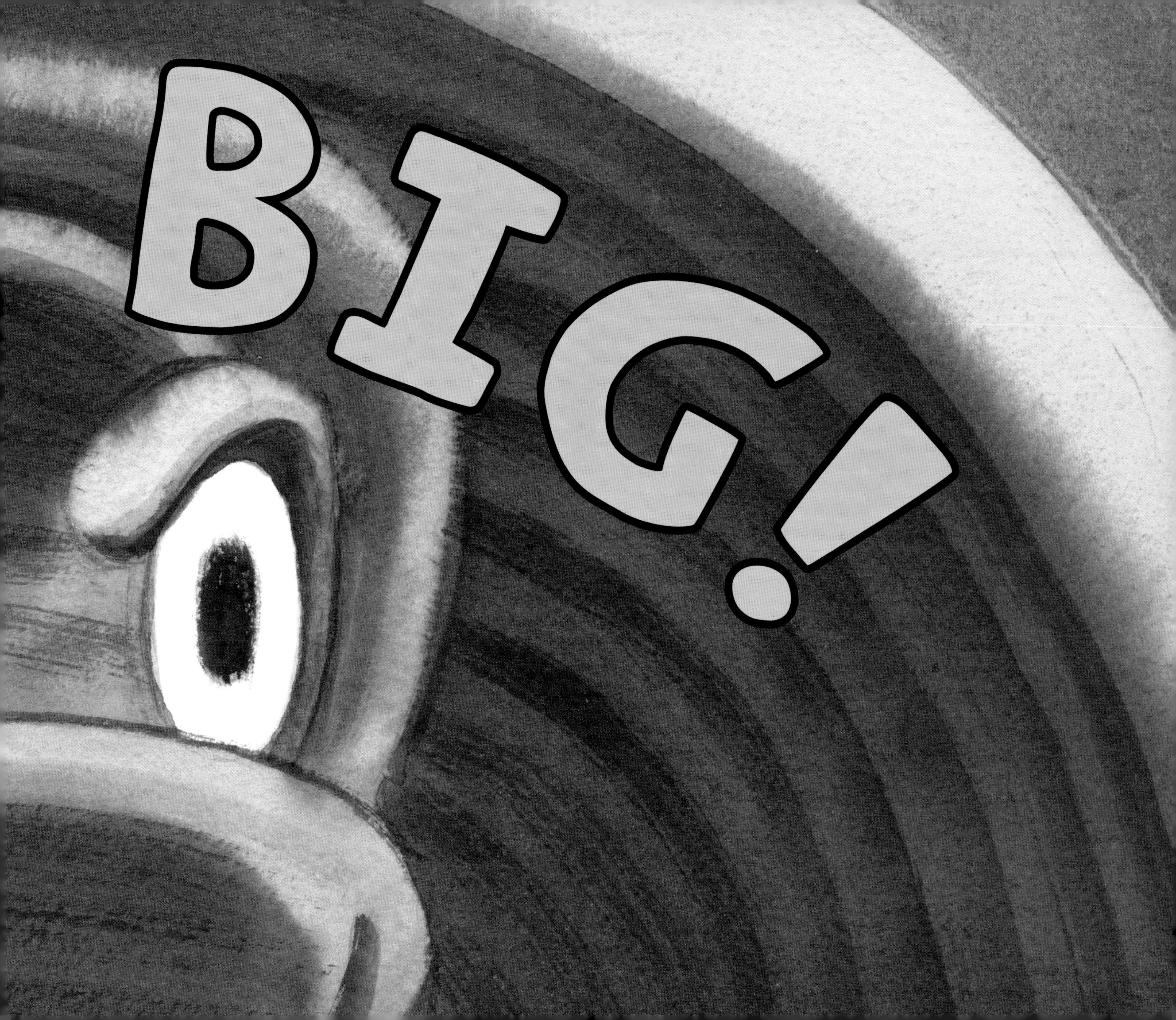
BIG!

... as the sun goes down.

Tomorrow morning?
I'm up with the birdies—
TWEET!